FLY GUY'S NINJA CHRISTMAS

Tedd Arnold

Cartwheel Books

An Imprint of Scholastic Inc.

Merry Christmas to
Huey and Damion

Library of Congress Cataloging-in-Publication Data

Names: Arnold, Tedd, author, illustrator. | Arnold, Tedd. Fly Guy ; 16.
Title: Fly Guy's ninja Christmas / Tedd Arnold.
Description: First edition. | New York : Cartwheel Books, an imprint of Scholastic Inc., 2016. | © 2016 | Series: Fly Guy ; 16 |
Summary: It is Christmas Eve and Fly Guy realizes that he does not have a present to give to his best friend, Buzz — but when he looks around the house searching for something suitable he discovers a stranger in a red suit, and decides to attack with some ninja moves.
Identifiers: LCCN 2015048862 | ISBN 9780545662772
Subjects: LCSH: Santa Claus — Juvenile fiction. | Flies — Juvenile fiction. | Pets — Juvenile fiction. | Best friends — Juvenile fiction. | Christmas stories. | CYAC: Santa Claus — Fiction. | Flies — Fiction. | Pets — Fiction. | Best friends — Fiction. | Friendship — Fiction. | Christmas — Fiction. | Humorous stories. | GSAFD: Humorous fiction.
Classification: LCC

PZ7.A7379 Fr 2016 | DDC 813.54 — dc23
LC record available at http://lccn.loc.gov/2015048862

10 9 8 7 6 5 4 3 2 1   16 17 18 19 20 21

Printed in China   38
First edition, October 2016
Book design by Steve Ponzo

A boy had a pet fly.
He named him Fly Guy.
Fly Guy could say the
boy's name —

Chapter 1

One night, Buzz was reading to Fly Guy. "...And the ninja saved the day."

"The end! That was a good book," said Buzz.

"Okay," said Buzz. "Time to sleep. Tomorrow is Christmas."

"Yes," said Buzz.
"Santa comes, and we
give each other presents."

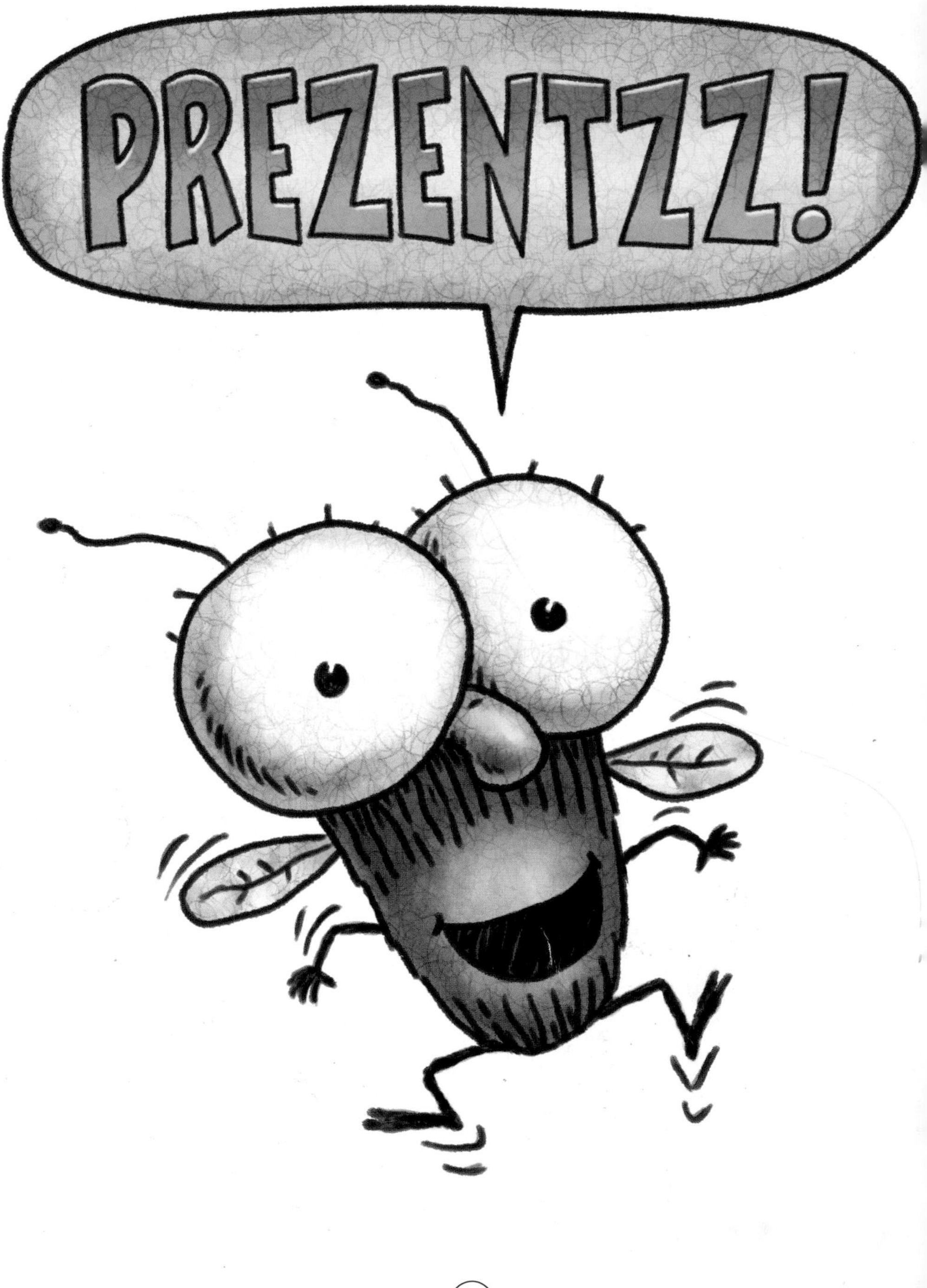
PREZENTZZ!

"Yes," said Buzz,
"now go to sleep."

Chapter 2

Fly Guy could not sleep. He did not have a present for Buzz. He went looking for one.

Fly Guy saw stockings on the fireplace. He saw a tree in the living room.

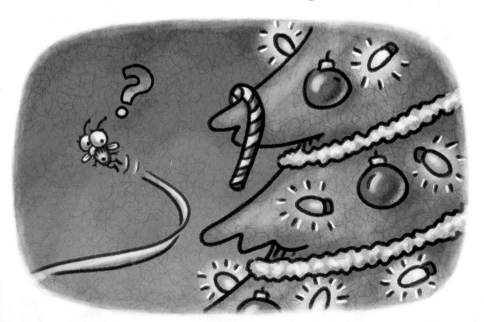

Fly Guy did not find a present to give Buzz. But he did find milk and cookies.

"Ho! Ho! Ho!" said a voice.
"I see you are eating my
cookies."

Fly Guy saw a big stranger in the house! He had to save the day.

Fly Guy went into ninja action!

"I heard something," said Buzz. **"SANTA CLAUS!"**

"Merry Christmas, Buzz," said Santa. "Will you and Fly Guy help me with the tree?"

They fixed the tree, then they all had milk and cookies. Buzz went back to bed.

Fly Guy said to Santa —

"Maybe I can help," said Santa.

Chapter 3

In the morning, Buzz woke up. "That was a cool dream," he said.

Buzz rushed to the tree.
He tore into his presents.

Finally, Buzz had only one
more small present to open.

The tag on the present reads: "To BUZZ FROM Fly Guy"

"Wait a minute," said Buzz.
"I haven't seen Fly Guy.
Where is he?"

"Fly Guy!" said Buzz. "You are the best present ever! What else is in here?"

"Wow! Who helped you get me this cool ninja suit?" said Buzz.

"Santa? I thought he was just a dream," said Buzz. "Here's my present for you, Fly Guy."